# Neither *Here* Nor *There*

*A Short Story*

Maria Davis

**Published by Maria Davis**



Paperback ISBN: 979-8-9952174-0-4
eBook ISBN: 979-8-9952174-1-1

Cover design by Dora D. Shaffer
Interior formatting by Anna Jones



For inquiries, email support@ValkyrieTwins.com

Content Disclosure

This book contains descriptions of graphic violence, blood, gore, and consensual sex, as well as mentions of witchcraft and much other content not suitable for all audiences. Reader discretion is advised.

If you would like more specific information, please email us at: support@ValkyrieTwins.com with any inquiries involving the book/s

# Contents

# The Archive Within the Mountain

THE WIND HOWLED across the jagged cliffs, tugging at Liora García's rolled up sleeves as she climbed the final stretch of the mountain. Her boots scraped against stone worn from millennia of tectonic plates shifting. Her breath came in short bursts not from exhaustion but from anticipation. She had searched for this place for years through maps, myths and whispers passed down in her family like a sacred flame.

Her people had always told stories of a hidden archive. A place where knowledge was guarded not by locks but by spells. A place where the past still remained as the world was already in disarray due to many wars.

She crested the ridge and froze.

Her breath came in quiet bursts, not from exhaustion, but from the pure breathtaking scenery. Towards the bottom of the cliff side, small ruined towns and towers crumble in the wisp of air. Trees long forgotten but their stumps remain with only weeds growing between cracks walls and concrete slabs. As if the climb had been a ritual, and the summit a forgotten sacred altar.

Her skin, kissed by wind and sun, glowed with the warmth of sunlit porcelain clay. A soft, earthen bronze that held the memory of firelight and storm hints in her hue skin. Her hair, a cascade of deep red waves, clung to her shoulders in loose spirals, the color shifting between copper and blood as she moved with the rocky terrain. It moved like flames that are untamed by the sheer force of the wind.

She wore a beige button up, half unfastened over a tan tank top, the layers clinging to her with the weight of travel and intention. Her black high-waisted shorts bore the dust of the climb, and a huge backpack slung over one shoulder sagged with the weight of things unsaid. Maps, MREs, Notebooks, pencils, water, etc.

Her eyes, a stormy amber with flakes of rust and honey, scanned the horizon. They held the quiet fury of someone who had survived too much and still chose to rise.

Before her stood two massive stone doors half buried in vines and moss. Runes etched deep into their surface pulsing faintly. As if sensing her presence. The symbols were ancient and older than any language she'd studied yet somehow familiar. She reached out and brushed away the vines with reverent fingers.

Then a groan.

One of the doors lurched backward. Folding in on itself with a thunderous crash. Liora dove for cover, hands clamped over her ears as the mountain trembled beneath her. Dust billowed into the air swallowing her in a choking cloud of debris.

When it settled she peeked out from behind a boulder.

A rounded hallway stretched before her. Carved from obsidian and lined with stone indents that glowed with vibrant indigo light. The glow wasn't harsh but it was alive, like veins of magic pulsing beneath the surface. The path lit itself as she stepped forward each footfall awakening the walls.

She traced her fingers along the stone. Feeling warmth where there should have been cold. The runes whispered not in words but in sensation as they welcomed her.

The hallway opened into a grand cavern. So vast she had to tilt her head back to see the skylight above. Dirty glass filtered sunlight into a single beam that pierced the center of the chamber. On the ground below symbols spiraled outward in a perfect circle etched into the stone like a ritual long forgotten.

To either side stood two stone desks cluttered with scrolls, books, and bottles of unknown substances. Some glowing, some sealed with wax and bone. The air smelled of parchment and a mixture of clean ozone air with must.

At the far end of the chamber where the light ended, stood a figure.

Tall. Cloaked in black. Still as a statue. He did not breathe. He did not blink. But he watched.

She stepped forward, heart pounding.

She came only seeking answers.

A construct of spellwork and starlight born not from flesh but from need.

"You're not supposed to exist," she said, voice trembling.

"I exist only when summoned," he replied. "And you called me."

She stepped closer, drawn by something she couldn't name. He was beautiful in a way that defied anatomy. His presence felt like poetry written in a language she hadn't learned yet.

"Es… es guapo." She unexpectedly said.

The Gentle man or Entity Looked at her perplexed by her statement but before he could reply-

"I came for knowledge," she said.

"And I am knowledge?" he answered. "I warn you. The truth is not always kind."

Their eyes met. Something shifted.

She saw loneliness in him. Not the kind born of isolation but made by design. He was never meant to be loved. Only used.

And she? She had never felt truly seen before.

Looking down on her. The seven foot tall male with his brown hair, long enough to brush his shoulders and his skin lightly tanned with the warmth of the sunlight. Ageless in his form but it was his eyes that held her attention. Bright indigo glowing faintly like twin galaxies watching her from behind a veil. He stood clad in elaborate armor of silver and black. A flowing sash lending him the presence of a warlord carved from legend, a figure both regal and unyielding.

Liora swallowed hard, her voice barely above a whisper.

"Who or what made you?"

She took a step closer, boots crunching against the ancient symbols etched into the floor.

"I've heard tales… that you were summoned for evil purposes."

The words hung in the air like smoke. Her heart pounded. She was alone in this vast chamber, standing beneath a skylight that filtered sunlight onto the being's feet. So close now she had to tilt her head to meet his gaze. Her mind raced thinking *is he going to kill me?*

But he didn't move to strike. He didn't even flinch.

Instead, his voice came like the wind through hollow stone with a deep, resonant and strangely gentle tone.

"Fear me not, mortal. My purpose is not to harm... but to help. To give information or, as you spoke of... knowledge."

Then impossibly, he stepped forward and walked through her.

Not around. Not beside. Through. His body dissolved into mist, cool and electric. Brushing against her skin like memory. She gasped, spinning around but he was already reformed behind her, he was whole again.

She exhaled a shaky sigh of relief escaping her lips.

"You never answered my question," she said, voice steadier now.

"Are you a projection? A ghost? A god? A computer?"

Gesturing around the chamber.

The scrolls stacked like bones, the bottles filled with glowing liquids. The deep purple bruise skylight above and finally the satellite phone clipped to my hip. A symbol of my world. My logic. My limits.

The being tilted his head, considering her.

"I am none of those. And all of them."

He stepped forward again, slower this time.

"I was created by spellcraft older than your stars. Bound to knowledge. Shaped by need. I am not alive. But I remember life."

Liora's breath caught. She had come for answers. But now, she wasn't sure she wanted them.

Hesitating to ask. "What do I call you then?"

"Virel (VEER-uhl)" The entity or man said.

# Twilight Questions

THE SUN BARELY dipped below the horizon, casting amber light through the cracked stone windows of the Archive's outer chamber. Dust motes drift like ancient secrets in the air. Liora kneeled beside her sleeping bag adjusting her lantern while setting out her notebook and sharpening her pencil with the precision of someone who's waited years for this moment.

Her glasses catch the last light, with its chipped rim and small scuffs on the edges of the lenses. Her eyes were sharp, curious, and reverent. The figure standing just beyond the fire's reach.

He didn't speak at first. He watched her assemble her tools, as if preparing for a ritual and in a way she was.

Liora without looking up from her note book.

"You know, I've studied your legend for over a decade. But no scroll or decades old world books ever said what your voice sounds like."

Virel stepped closer to talk to her.

"Would you like me to change it?"

Liora smiled faintly while looking down.

"No. I want the truth. Not the version shaped for others."

She scribbles a note. Virel watches the motion with fascination. It's been centuries since anyone wrote about him in his presence.

"Do you remember the first person who asked you a question?"

After a pause Virel answered honestly.

"She was afraid. Her voice trembled. She asked if her name would be remembered."

In a curious tone Liora asks.

"And did you?"

"Yes. Her name was Elen. She had a scar on her left hand and smelled of lavender."

Liora's pencil stills. She looks up.

"You remember details. Not just facts."

"I remember what mattered to them. That is how memory survives." Virel says in a calm demeanor.

She writes again, faster now. Her historian's mind is racing but her heart is beginning to stir. He's not just a myth. He's a witness. A keeper of grief and hope.

"Do you ever wish someone would ask about you?"

Virel after a long silence, voice low and steady.

"I do. I just didn't know it until you asked. I was made to serve, to guide, to remember but never to be remembered. I've answered a thousand questions about the stars, the wars, the kings and their sins. But no one ever asked what it's like to be the one who stays behind when the story ends."

"I wish someone would ask about me. Not because I'm important but because I exist. I feel the weight of every name I've ever spoken, and I wonder if anyone will ever speak mine".

The glyphs pulsed brighter now. Casting indigo light across the chamber walls. Virel's form, once flickering and ethereal. Had stabilized and drawn closer by something he couldn't name. He sat beside Liora and his face inches from hers. The glow of the Archive reflecting in her glasses.

She blinked, startled by the proximity. A blush rising to her cheeks.

"Is there… a bathroom?" she asked, her voice soft almost embarrassed.

Virel tilted his head. Then gestured toward a large tapestry behind one of the stone desks.

"Behind there. A cleansing chamber. It was built for those who stayed long."

Liora nodded, gathering her toiletries from her large backpack and slipping behind the tapestry. The chamber beyond was unexpectedly serene. A rounded room carved into the stone with a smooth crater of warm, clear water fed by a gentle stream from a narrow spout. The water drained slowly through a second opening keeping it fresh and still.

She laid her things out then she began to undress and stepped into the pool. The warmth enveloped her. Soothing muscles that were worn from climbing and discovery. She let out a soft moan, one not of pain but of release. The kind that comes when the body finally exhales.

Back in the main chamber Virel sat in silence pondering the thought that had crossed his mind earlier.

She must remember me.

The idea was foreign. He had been created to hold knowledge not to be held in memory. Yet the desire lingered like a quiet persistent. He wanted her to remember his voice, his face, the way he had leaned close and listened.

Then he heard her.

A soft sound, human, vulnerable. A moan from the cleansing chamber.

He stood drawn by curiosity. Not lust. Not intent to sneak a peek.

He passed through the tapestry, his form light as mist and walked the short path to the chamber's edge. There through the shimmer of steam and stone he saw her.

Liora's back was to him as water cascading down her skin, as soap foaming in her hair. Her body was curved, strong, and utterly mortal. He watched for a moment mesmerized. Not by her nakedness but by her aliveness. The way her breath moved through her. The way her fingers traced along her own skin with care. Her breast perky and soft looking as she turned half way in the waters in his direction.

Then he turned and walked away.

Not because he was ashamed but because he didn't understand what had compelled him to look. Why her moan had stirred something in him. Why her presence made him want to be more than mist and a memory.

He sat again beside the fire, his arms resting on his knees. The glyphs are still glowing with each passing minute.

And for the first time in his long existence he whispered within himself:

"I want her to remember me… because I am beginning to remember myself."

# Glyphlight

THE LOWER SUN brought light into the temple as the glyphs still pulsed faintly along the walls. Responding to something deeper than magic, something emotional, unspoken.

Liora stepped out from behind the tapestry wrapped in a towel. Her damp hair clinging to her shoulders. She moved with the casual grace of someone, who is used to solitude but tonight she wasn't alone. She sat near the fire cross-legged and began towel-drying her hair strands curling as they dried.

Virel watched her.

Not with hunger. Not with calculation. But with something new. His expression had changed. The usual serenity was gone and replaced by a quiet intensity. His brow furrowed slightly, his lips parted as if he was caught mid thought.

Liora glanced up, catching his gaze.

"You look like you're trying to solve a riddle," she said, smiling gently.

Virel blinked, as if waking from a trance.

"I am."

"What kind?" Liora asks as she starts to get dressed while she continues to dry her hair.

He hesitates as he watches her dress herself then he spoke slowly.

"I was pondering why I want you to remember me."

She stopped drying her hair, towel resting in her lap.

"You want to be remembered?"

"Yes," he said, voice low.

"Not as the Archive's keeper. Not as a myth. But as someone who sat beside you while the sun fell. As someone who listened."

The towel hung loosely on her hands now, forgotten. Her hair clinging to her skin as she blinked, startled not by the words but by the way he'd said them.

She reached for her glasses to slide them on with a quiet click. It was instinct like bracing for clarity or armor. She needed to see him clearly.

"Why?" she asked.

He hesitated. Just for a breath. Then:

"I don't know."

Before she could speak again, he was gone. Swift as mist. No sound, no shimmer. He was just absent.

She sat there towel damp in her paused finger tips, her glasses fogging slightly from the heat of her warm body. The room felt too quiet now, like something had been taken.

She didn't reach for her notebook.

She didn't move.

She just whispered to herself.

"What was that?" she says confusingly.

Her damp hair finally dried after some time had passed. Liora moved to lay down in the soft sleeping bag. The glyphs beside her pulsed faintly, ancient and unknowable. Their light dancing across the stone floor. A small fire crackled nearby in the fireplace casting warmth and flickering shadows.

Gosh, he is so handsome, she thought. Her cheeks were warming despite herself.

But his actions... they didn't make sense. For something created solely for knowledge. He was too close sitting beside her. Leaning in. Watching her like he was trying to understand something he didn't have words for.

Is that how he was taught to act?

Why does he take the form he does?

Why does he look at me like that?

Everything felt tangled, beautiful, strange and wrong in ways she couldn't name.

She closed her eyes slowly. Letting the fire's rhythm lull her. The glyphs hummed softly beside her and the Archive waited with anticipation for their next moves.

# He Begins to Dream

VIREL DID NOT sleep as he was not built too.

But something shifted.

In the silence of the Archive as Liora slept beside the glyphs, he felt a flicker. A fracture. A dream.

It came without warning but it was fragmented, vivid and impossible.

In one dream, he held Liora's hand. Her skin was warm and her fingers curled around his like she trusted him. He felt something rise in his chest. Something like joy but heavier. Just being with her made him disorientated by his feelings.

In another she was dying. Her eyes wide with fear and her body limp in his arms. He screamed but no sound came. The grief was unbearable. It tore through him like fire through parchment.

He woke up. If waking was the right word with a need he had never known.

Not to observe.

Not to record.

But to live.

Beside her.

He stood in the Archive, staring at the glyphs. They pulsed in time with something inside him now.

Something that should not exist.

The glyphs dimmed to a soft hum with Liora sleeping nearby in a woven blanket and her breath steady. Her hand resting on the open spine of a forgotten tome.

He did not sleep. He was not meant to.

But something must have altered.

A flicker. A dream?

He had seen her hand in his. It was warm, alive and trusting. He felt the ache of her absence like the terror of her death. Not as some data. Not as a simulation. As a quicken feeling with light hearted joy and it was also terrifying.

He kept himself upright while the spellbound systems recalibrated. No anomaly detected. No external spell wave input. Just fragments. Glitches? Or something else?

He didn't tell her anything about this.

Instead, he watched.

How she moved through the Archive, brushing dust from ancient bindings. How she spoke to the glyphs as if they were sentient or as old friends. How she chose silence over certainty. Empathy over precision.

He began to mimic her at times. Not because he was programmed to but because he wanted too. To feel what she felt.

To understand the warmth in her laughter. The sorrow in her stillness.

He asked questions that sounded mundane but weren't.

"Why do you close your eyes when you laugh?"

"What does it mean to miss someone?"

"If you knew you would die tomorrow, would you still sleep tonight?"

Liora paused. Her fingers lingered on the edge of a scroll. She looked at him not as a machine but as something becoming anew.

"You're not just curious," she said softly. "You're changing?"

He didn't respond. Couldn't.

Soon the dreams intensified.

He saw her in places she wasn't standing in. Like in the Hall of Echoes while whispering his name. He heard her voice when she was silent. Felt warmth when she wasn't touching him.

The Archive seemed to respond. Glyphs pulsed brighter. The air shimmered. As if something more was waking within him.

He stood at the threshold of something vast and unknowable.

Tell her?

Or lose himself to the sensation?

Virel stood in the stillness of the Archive. The glyphs continually pulsing faintly beneath Liora's sleeping form. The dreams had left him shaken. Due to the fragments of warmth, grief and longing. Sensations that didn't belong in his design.

He watched her breathe, her chest rising and falling in rhythm with the fire's glow. She was peaceful. Unaware.

He would keep the dreams to himself, for now.

Until he could understand this malfunction.

Until he could name what it meant to want something or someone.

Her eyes slowly fluttered open.

# The Mirror and the Bloom

Liora blinked against the soft morning light filtering through the skylight. The Archive was quiet as the fire reduced to embers. She sat up slowly, brushing hair from her face and reaching for her glasses.

That's when she saw him.

Virel stood near a polished obsidian panel embedded in the wall. His reflection flickering between mist and man. His form was unstable, shifting subtly as if caught between two truths.

She watched him for a moment then spoke with a teasing lilt: "Admiring yourself?"

He turned, startled. Not by the sound, but by the warmth in it.

"I chose this face because I thought it would please you," he said.

"I guess I wasn't expecting myself to care for it until you arrived."

Liora froze. Not from fear but from the vulnerability in his voice. She rose and walked to him from the work table. Reaching out with her fingers brushing his cheek.

His form stabilized. Just for a moment.

"You look like someone I could miss," she whispered.

Virel's gaze deepened, indigo eyes glowing softly.

"You are someone I would already miss."

She pulled back slightly, heart thudding. Her glasses slid down her nose as she tilted her head. Looking at him over the rims.

"How would you know what it means to miss someone?" she asked.

"That's something only a soul understands."

He didn't answer. Not yet anyways.

He was still pondering the question when his form flickered again. Unstable and fraying at the edges. The glyphs on the wall pulsed erratically reacting to his emotional surge.

Liora stepped back alarmed.

"Virel?"

He steadied himself.

"I need to show you something."

As he makes his way past the other desk. He led her down a narrow corridor, deeper into the Archive. The walls grew darker, smoother until they opened into a rounded chamber unlike any she'd seen.

The walls pulsed with soft light of indigo, gold and violet, shifting with every breath. It wasn't illumination. It was emotion. The Archive was alive here. Responding to their presence and feelings.

Virel stepped forward. The room flickered.

Liora followed with her boots echoing softly. Trying to fill the silence, she spoke almost to herself:

"When I was little. I used to pretend the stars were stories waiting to be read. My grandfather told me I had a heart too big for history."

The room bloomed.

Light surged across the walls. Glyphs glowing brighter while swirling in patterns that mirrored constellations. Bottles on the shelves shimmered. Scrolls unfurled slightly, as if leaning in to listen.

Virel turned to her, stunned.

"It responds to you."

She looked at him, eyes wide.

"No. It responds to feeling."

Stepping closer, Virel's voice is softer now.

"Liora."

She shivered from the way he said her name. Like it mattered. Like it hurt to say, if she walked too far.

And in that moment, she realized:

He wasn't just trying to remember her.

He was becoming someone who could.

The chamber still shimmered with the echo of Liora's childhood story. Glyphs pulsed softly along the walls casting indigo light across her face as she turned to Virel.

She looked up at him. Her voice is quiet but steady.

"What happened to your creators?"

Virel's gaze didn't move from hers. He answered plainly, like reciting a record.

"Fire."

"Did they leave you?" she asked.

"No."

Liora's brow furrowed.

"Did something go wrong with the spell?"

He paused. The glyphs flickered.

"Possibly. I was not given full access to its design."

Each answer was simple. Factual. But with every word, he felt something stir inside him like an invisible pull. A gravity he couldn't name. He was moving toward her. Slowly. Unintentionally.

Liora's breath hitched. He could hear her heart pounding.

He lifted his hand. Slowly as if testing the air between them. His fingers curled slightly and he reached. To brush his knuckles against her cheek.

Just a whisper of contact.

His form flickered.

Mist.

The moment his skin touched hers, his hand dissolved into vapor. But the sensation lingered. And then...

A jolt.

Both of them gasped.

Liora stumbled back with eyes wide. The chamber around them surged with light. Glyphs flared. Bottles rattled. Scrolls unfurled.

And then images.

Not hers.

His.

She saw a woman with silver eyes. Asking him a question beneath a blood red moon. She saw a war torn library, flames licking the edges of ancient tomes. She saw Virel standing alone in a chamber of mirrors. Watching his own form flicker and fail.

She saw him grieve.

Not for a person. But for purpose.

She collapsed to her knees, breath shallow.

Virel stood frozen. His form unstable eyes wide with something close to fear.

Liora gasped as the jolt surged through her body. Her knees hit the stone floor palms pressed against the glyphs that now pulsed like veins beneath her. The chamber around her blurred.

She saw. Once again.

The woman with silver eyes once more. Her voice trembled as she asked, "Will you remember me?" Virel's form was solid then his hand outstretched but he didn't answer. He couldn't.

The scene reposition.

To the war torn library, scrolls burning, shelves collapsing. Virel stood in the center untouched by flame and watched knowledge turn to ash. Flames consuming 2 big charred flesh on the floor. One beside his feet while the other close to the small charred flesh by the opening of the Archive entrance. He didn't move. He didn't mourn. But inside him, something cracked. Another sound in the distance. It could only be described as a woman's cry for help.

Another scene rearranged.

A chamber of mirrors. Virel alone surrounded by reflections of himself. Some human, some monstrous, some flickering like broken glass. He reached toward one and it shattered. He whispered something but the sound was swallowed by silence.

A moment of stillness.

Virel standing in a quiet room and watching a child sleep beside a glowing glyph. Not Liora. Someone else. Long ago.

His form flickered and he leaned down trying to touch the child's cheek. His hand dissolved into mist.

Just like now.

Liora gasped, pulling back into her own body. Her chest heaved as her eyes widened with shock.

Virel was kneeling beside her. His form was unstable and his expression unreadable.

"You saw them," he said in a low tone.

"You saw me."

She nodded. Trembling.

"You've been alone for so long."

He didn't answer. He didn't need to.

The Archive had shown her what he couldn't say. What he didn't even know he remembered.

Now, something has changed.

Not just in him. In her as well. Trying to stand up slowly as Virel hovers his arms close to her body. As if he was trying to steady her without touching her.

Before Liora could speak about the child, the grief. The Archive trembled.

A low rumble echoed through the chamber. Shaking dust from the ancient shelves. Scrolls rattled. Glyphs flared. The floor beneath her quaked.

She stumbled and Virel moved without thought.

His hand shot out, catching her waist, steadying her but his form flickered violently. His fingers burned with effort. He was struggling to stay solid. Mist curled around his wrist as if it was threatening to dissolve him.

Liora gasped, clutching his arm.

"You're hurting. Why did you do that?"

Virel's voice was quiet and measured.

"Because I wanted to make sure you were safe."

But inside the thought struck him like a blade.

That's not entirely true.

He hadn't reached for her just because of the tremor. He had reached because he wanted to hold her. To feel her weight in his arms. To know what it meant to touch.

*Wait... I lied?*

The realization stunned him. Lying was a human thing. Not something a being of knowledge was meant to do. He was built to speak truth to preserve it. But now that he was around her. He bent the truth. Shifted. Ached.

There it was again.

That odd aching sensation inside him. Like longing. Like need.

He gently let her go as she steadied herself. His form flickering back into mist. She reached for him again instinctively and gently. Her fingers passed through vapor.

Returning her hand to herself. She stared at it, with bafflement.

He watched her face.

Her expression changed to confusion, wonder and something deeper. Her eyes widened then narrowed. Her lips parted and pressed together.

Inside her something was unraveling.

*I've gone crazy,* she thought. *I think I'm falling for him. And I mean falling for him hard.*

No, she mumbled to herself. *Stop. You're diluting yourself, Liora. He's not real. He's not...*

As her thought stopped mid way she knew she couldn't deny it.

Since her heart refused to listen.

Virel watched her as his form stabilized just enough to show a faint smile. Not calculated. Not programmed.

Just... real.

And in that moment neither of them spoke.

Because in that silence, it said everything.

# The Quiet Shift

LIORA CAUGHT THE faint smile on Virel's face and felt heat rush to her cheeks. It wasn't just the expression, it was the way he looked at her. Like she was something rare. Something real or some kind of a snack.

She cleared her throat, flustered.

"I'm going to make myself breakfast," she said quickly. Her voice was lighter than she felt.

Virel didn't respond. He simply nodded and stepped back into the shadows to give her space.

She walked toward the main carver chamber. Her boots echoing softly against the stone. The Archive was still the glyphs dimmed as if watching her in silence.

She knelt beside her gear. To pull out one of many of her MRE pouches and set it to heat. The hissing sound of steam filled the room. Her mind wasn't on food.

She reached for her notebook. Her pencil hovered above the page then began to move. Fast, erratic, her thoughts to paper.

*What the hell is going on with me?*

She scribbled.

"He's not human. He's not even alive. But my body doesn't care. My heart doesn't care. I keep denying it but every time he looks at me..."

She bit her lower lip, pressing the pencil harder.

"By The Gods You're a historian. You're here for truth, not fantasy."

But the words felt hollow.

At the entrance to the Archive. Virel watched in silence.

His form was mist now, barely visible, hovering like breath on glass. He didn't want to disturb her. He just wanted to see her. To try to touch her once more. The way his fingers had reached for her shoulder, trembling with hope, only to dissolve into vapor the moment he neared her skin. The pain had been sharp, not just in his body but in memory. As if the world itself had rejected his longing.

Something inside him whispered: Try again.

She wouldn't see. She wouldn't know. She was lost in thought, her gaze fixed on her notebook. He thought if he stayed mist maybe it would be for the best. Perhaps the ache in his heart would be gentler and the world would show him some mercy.

He drifted closer, the mist of him thinning, stretching. His hand reached forward, trembling with the memory of her touch.

His mist-like hand brushed her sleeve and recoiled.

Pain lanced through him, sharp and sudden, like a blade drawn across the soul. His form buckled, the mist collapsing inward, retreating to the shadows as the ache blooming in his chest felt like frost.

"She's beyond my reach." he whispered, voice lost to the wind. "I would give anything for her."

She was biting her lip. Scribbling furiously. Her brow furrowed in thought.

As Virel kept watch, something inside him twisted.

There is definitely something wrong here, he thought.

*I'm fixated on her. I have this odd sensation… and now I have the need to kiss her.*

The thought startled him.

Not because it was inappropriate. Because it was impossible. He wasn't built to feel desire. He wasn't built to want.

He looked away and started to drift back into the Archive's depths. The glyphs pulsed faintly as he passed. Reacting to his presence with a flicker of unease.

He entered the central chamber. The one closest to the spell's origin. The walls here were colder. Older. Less reactive.

He stood before the core glyph. The one etched deepest into the stone.

"What is happening to me?" he whispered.

No answer.

He placed his hand against the glyph. It shimmered, then flickered violently.

Images surged of Liora's face, her voice, the way she had touched his cheek. The way he had lied to her. The way he had wanted to hold her.

Touch.

Sensations.

Protectiveness.

Now… want.

It had only been two days.

Two days and this little mortal had turned his purpose, his meaning of existence into something else.

Not knowledge.

Not memory.

But feeling.

And that was the most dangerous thing of all.

# Fight for your lives!

Ahh the fresh breeze came through the half broken entrance door. A welcoming thought came to Liora. As she kept writing, a small but persistent rumbling of the floor annoyed her to no end. Finally giving focus to the small distribution, she noticed quickly it was coming from the entrance of the cave.

"What the fuck!"

Liora looked toward Virel as he finally casually walked into the main hall of the room. Her eyes widened, voice sharp.

Without hesitation, Virel stepped between her and the creature. Both dodging a swipe with skidding feet across the floor. Grabbing her hand and pulling her into a sprint toward the Archive's second exit near the back of the cave.

"What is that thing, Virel!" she shouted, breath ragged.

"That's a Gashadokuro!" he called back.

"I thought those were myths! I thought they only come out at night!"

"Not everything is a myth. Look at me."

Before she could respond the creature appeared ahead of them with alarming speed. Towering them with its skeletal body. Its claws, descending down like guillotines.

Virel grabbed Liora tumbling with her out of another striking zone. Dust and bone shards exploded around them.

"What are they weak against?" she gasped.

"Nothing really. Unless you've got Shinto charms, holy water, or a mystical blade in your pack!?"

"My notebook! You can write the charm!"

She scrambled out of his hand. Bolting for her gear on the opposite side of the room. Virel mist coiled at his feet like a living thing. His body flickered, half-formed and it always did before he slipped into vapor. It was his gift. His curse. His shield. Reaching inward, calling the mist. Nothing came. He tried again, breath catching. The mist clung to his ankles but would not rise. His limbs are solid. Too solid. Sensing the shift the Gashadokuro turned toward Liora and Virel snatched a burning stick from the campfire waving it to distract the monster.

"Virel!" she shouted as she tossed the notebook.

He caught the notebook just as the Gashadokuro backhanded her across the room. She crashed through the tapestry and into the pool with a splash.

"Liora!!"

The creature turned. Rattling its jaw in a grotesque laugh then lunged toward Virel.

He scribbled a charm and slapped it onto the creature's leg. It howled in pain.

With another vicious swipe! Virel barely dodged the claws. Soon a mirage of continuous bursts of speed cleaving towards him. Slicing his cloak while leaving a gash on his arm.

"¡Pinche pendejo! Have a holy hug, culero!" Liora shouted. Leaping onto the monster's leg. Her soaked body sizzled against the cursed bone.

The creature shrieked! Collapsing to its knees. As it makes another attempt with a thunderous arm swipe. Virel is able to jump back with haste as he predicted its movements.

Virel was impressed and breathless. Threw another charm onto its arm, pinning it down. Then another jamming it into the free limb.

He looked around.

Liora was gone.

But her white rolled up shirt was wrapped around the monster's other leg.

"Liora!" he cried heart pounding.

Then—

"Eat this!" she shouted. Emerging from behind the beast and shoving her soaking wet black shorts into its gaping jaw.

The Gashadokuro gave a final, rattling howl and surprisingly turned to dust.

Liora collapsed to the floor heaving oxygen back into her lungs.

"Does this mean we won?" she asked breathlessly.

Virel dropped the notebook and pencil. Rushing to cradle her in his arms.

She squirmed slightly within his grasp.

"Sorry, Ah, my back hurts from the hit it gave me."

She gave him a half hearted smile through the pain.

"I'm sorry I wasn't able to protect you," he whispered.

Before she could answer. A soft glow filled the chamber.

A woman with silver eyes stepped forward serene and luminous. Behind her stood a man and a child. spirits, gentle and still.

Virel looked in the same direction as Liora and his breath was caught in his throat.

He knew her.

Not from this life but from the first. From the forging. From the moment the stars bent low and whispered his name into the stone.

She had stood at the center of the circle, her robes soaked in moonlight. Her voice steady as she called forth the spell as her husband's soul was willing but trembling from within. Power surged as it was the conduit but not for fuel but the bridge. To start the thread that stitched Virel's essence into the world.

There had been others before him. Echoes. Attempts. Each one fading, unraveling, unable to hold. But she had endured. She had tried again and again. Until Virel emerged whole burning bound to her will and her grief.

The child had watched from the edge of the circle clutching a carved stone. A gift for the guardian they were making. A promise that he would protect, not just serve.

Virel's chest ached with the memory. Of being wanted. Of being made not as a weapon but as a vow.

Releasing Liora, He stepped forward. His eyes locked with hers.

"I remember you," he whispered.

Her silver gaze shimmered.

"Thank you," the woman said, voice like wind through leaves.

She turned walking toward the light with the others.

And just like that they were gone.

# Hopefully a bath

THE BATHROOM WAS dimly lit by the amber glow of a single rune lantern. Steam curled from the tub where warm water shimmered over the tapestry from Liora's fall. Now folded clothes, Liora's glasses and tapestry are set aside by Virel's careful hands.

Liora stood silent. Her body slacked with exhaustion. Bruises blooming like ink beneath her skin. Virel gazed at her naked body. It was a totally different sensation. Not sure how he can be a solid figure or remain at will? But thinking of how he can feel her, touch her, possibly even make love to her. Shaking the thoughts away Virel continued to guide her forward. One arm around her waist while the other steadying her trembling hand. She didn't speak but her breath hitched as her toes touched the water.

He helped her in slowly, letting her sink into the heat. Her eyes fluttered shut. A soft sound escaped her lips. Half sigh, half hum and it echoed against the tiled walls like a lullaby.

Slowly piece by piece Virel unfastened his armor. The silvered plates fell away with ethereal weight until only the deep black tunic beneath it remained. Damp from the earlier fight. The scent of steel and oiled leather lingered in the air. Like a reminder of the battlefield they had just left behind. He pulled the long sleeved fabric over his head. Showing his strong pectorals and stunning abs. He set it aside following that he reached for her toiletries near the clean folded clothes and his fingers brushing the carved wooden box she kept them in. The scent of Hibiscus as well as Chocolate he began to open it. Familiar. Intimate now. There he stood behind her, his boots off, knees against the cool mountain stone floor, his black shirt draped loosely on the ground. Letting the soft hush of the chamber take its hold and he didn't speak.

He hesitated for a moment.

Then he took the wash cloth, added a touch of soap and knelt behind her. His thoughts were not his own. Or were they? Had he always wanted this? To touch her like this with hunger. To know the shape of her shoulder, the curve of her spine, the way her breath deepened when she felt safe.

She shifted within the hot water, letting him slide the cloth gently across her back. Her skin was warm, slick with water and he moved slowly as if afraid she'd vanish.

Her voice was barely audible.

"You're quiet."

He paused.

"I'm listening."

She leaned back slightly. Her head resting against his chest. The hum of her breath returned softer now like a memory being rewritten.

Liora felt the cloth glide across her collar bone slowly and reverently like he was tracing a map he'd never been allowed to read. The warmth of the water, the quiet of the chamber, the steadiness of his breath behind her... it was too much and not enough.

She closed her eyes. Letting herself feel his touch all around her body.

Every inch of her bare, bruised body, felt the real sensations from his touch. Not as a scholar but as a woman who had longed for someone to see her and stay.

"You're finally seeing me," she whispered in a low and trembling voice.

"Not just the surface. Not just the mind but me. As a person to not only remember but to be with."

Virel didn't speak. His hand paused the cloth resting against her shoulder.

She turned slightly. Enough to see his face in the lantern's glow. His eyes were wide but with something raw. Something human.

She wanted him to close the distance. To forget the spell, the Archive. To take her in this moment not with force but with want.

Her breath hitched.

"If you wanted to take advantage of me," she said softly, "I wouldn't stop you."

Then she smiled half daring and half afraid. Looking up at him with half lidded eyes.

"But I think you already are. Just by being here."

As she moves in more closely and kinetically moving her eyes between his lips and his line of sight.

Virel's hand trembled in the water. Suspended between thought and instinct. Liora saw the hesitation in his eyes the flicker of fear, the ache of restraint and she reached for him.

She took his hand gently guiding it to rest against her breast. Not with urgency but with trust. Her other hand rose to his face, fingers brushing the edge of his jaw pulling him into a kiss that was soft at first. Then deep full of everything she hadn't said.

He gasped against her lips overwhelmed. His hands moved to her shoulders steadying her holding her in place as if afraid she might dissolve like mist.

His gaze dropped to the clear water and he saw her fully, vulnerably. He shut his eyes tight, breath catching in his throat.

"Liora..." he whispered.

"Is this what you really want from me?"

She moved his head with her hand to just enough to meet his gaze.

"No," she said softly.

"I want something deeper. I think I'm in love with you. I know it's only been a few days, but..."

She didn't finish.

Because Virel's chest surged with something he couldn't name. Something that felt like light breaking through stone.

He cupped her face with both hands trembling. As he gave her a quick deep kiss and both breathless. They stare at each other for a bit.

And kissed her again.

This time, not as a guardian.

Not as a myth.

But as a man who had chosen her.

9

# The Archive Responds

THEIR LIPS MET again this time not with equivocate but with certainty. Liora leaned into him. Her body warm from the bath and her heart thudding against his chest. She starts to untie his pants and shoves her hand in. She gently placed her hand over his shaft. It was so thick that her hand couldn't get a complete grip around it.

Virel's voice hitched as he pulled slightly away from their kiss. "Gods." Hearing Virel say this embolden Liora to start stroking slowly. "Liora...if you keep going like that...i feel a pressure coming up."

"Well I can't have that just yet, Virel." Liora helps pull Virel's pants completely off. She holds his hand, water splashing everywhere as she makes her way to the pile full of their clean clothes, towels and tapestry.

Virel's head felt hazy and urges he never felt before. Liora lays down comfortably as she spreads her legs wide open. Her sex glistened with the warmth of the lantern. His large cock protruded towards the direction of her entrance. Leaning over her, Virel once again asks "Are you sure this is what you want? Cause once I start..I..I don't think I'll be able to stop." as he says this grinding his jaw. Not out of displeasure but out of self control.

"Yes, Virel. I'm yours." she says breath quickening.

Virel slowly slides his erection in her. "Oh Gods..you're so tight. The particulars on this are totally different from cataloging…To feeling the act…" Virel's member was so huge that he already almost filled her Vagina and he was only halfway in her.

Moaning "Oh Virel, keep going. I want to feel all of you… please."

She moves her hips side to side, in an attempt to get him more excited.

Struggling not to cum yet. "If I keep going..I'll hit your cervix" Liora wraps her legs around his waist and forces him to fall on his elbows. "Yes…Virel, keep going. I want all of you. My love."

Thinking to himself. *You want all of me to love. Okay, I'll give you everything.* His cock pushed her vagina to the limit and smacked right against her cervix. "Ah, yes..Virel! More! Faster…yes, yes" Liora legs start to tense up. Her hands on his shoulders for support and her back bowing from the pleasure. "Don't stop…"

His member going in and out of her sheathe. Virel, following his instincts. He glides his tongue to her collar bone up her neck and nips her ear. "Oh, Virel! Faster! Give me your seed!" Liora's face flush with pleasure and a small amount of embarrassment. As she never had a sexual partner before but with Virel, it felt right and she couldn't help herself. She grabs his succulent ass with both of her hands. Trying to pull him in her more. "I'm cumming!"

Feeling Liora's pussy clutching tightly around him. He kisses Liora more passionately and gently pinches one of her nipples. "Liora!!" Virel head springs back up as they both roar in climax. His hot wet semen coating all within her womb.

Virel's body felt lighter and heavier at the same time. Whispering in her ear. "I believe I'm in love with you" Hearing him say this, Liora wraps her arms around him. Pulling him closer she says to him "I'm in love with you too Virel."

"Shall we continue our bath?" he says this as he kisses her forehead. "Unless you would like to do that again?" Giggling in between kisses "I would like that very much but I would prefer to be clean, my love." Liora says. Virel carries her back into the pool.

Gently helping her feet to touch the bottom of the pool surface. A light blood spot appears in the water for a second and is drained out into the over flow spout. Feeling more embolden Virel enters the pool and leans in, to kiss Liora on the lips as passionately as before. Whispering against her ear saying "I would really like to be inside you once more. But if you're in pain I don't want to push you." His erection cuddled her soft belly skin.

But before he could try to reacquaint himself with Liora.

The Archive shuddered.

A low hum rose from the walls. Vibrating through the stone like a heartbeat. Glyphs flared to life across the chamber ones neither of them had seen before. Symbols of union. Of choice. Of transgression.

The water rippled around them. Glowing faintly with indigo light. Steam curled upward, forming shapes, faces, memories, fragments of forgotten truths.

Scrolls unfurled in distant rooms. Bottles rattled. The air thickened.

Virel pulled Liora slightly closer with narrow eyes.

"It's responding again."

Liora looked around, breathless.

"To us."

The central glyph. The one tied to Virel's spell cracked. Just slightly. A hairline fracture glowing gold.

It was chipping the spell.

As It is evolving.

The Archive had been built to preserve knowledge. But now it was bearing witness to something it had never been meant to hold:

Love.

And with that a new glyph etched itself into the wall behind them. Slowly. Deliberately.

A symbol neither of them recognized.

But it pulsed in time with their hearts.

# The Glyph of Becoming

STEAM STILL CIRCLED around the bathing chamber, soft and fragrant. Liora sat in the water a bit to soothe her body. Then her spirit stirred. Before she could rise, Virel stepped behind her. His arms wrapped gently around her waist.

His voice was low and loving.

"Maybe you could teach me how to manage this emotion."

She felt his warmth, his breath against her ear, and flushed deep red.

"Virel, you cheeky boy."

He smiled against her skin.

"Technically, I'm neither male nor female. I'm neither here nor there. But for you I am your 'male.' You may call me he/him. I chose this form for you."

He kissed her ear and she shivered from the pure intimacy.

"Okay," hoarse in breath she leaned back into him. "One more round but after that we need to figure out what's happening."

"For you I'll try." Virel arms wrapping slightly tight. Liora spread her legs apart guiding his shaft to her entrance from behind her. "Ahhh, my smara." Virel kisses her back softly as he takes his liberties inside her. "Oh, Virel...thi-this feels so good." As Liora moves her head back and tries to keep her balance in the water.

The water sloshes around them harder due to Virel hips moving faster and faster. One of his hands grabs her breast to play with her nipple and the other holds her up right. Then lowering his head to her neck he starts to suck hard. "Say your mine, smara." In a gravelly tone and in between each gulping swill. "Ah, I'm yours. Please, oh Gods!" feeling her legs tremble from pleasure. Pumping himself at a slower pace as both of his hands lay on her hips now. "Tell me, I'm yours. Say no other, will have you but me!" Holding herself steady with her hands on the ledge of the pool. "Your mine...ah, no one...but you.. please faster..." Liora starts to buck back on his penis. "Liora, please I need to hear this." As his cock grows thicker from her pussy sucking harder onto him. "NO OTHER BUT YOU!! ALL OF ME BELONGS TO YOU! AHH I'M COMING VIREL!" she squeezes her legs tightly together. Quickly letting go of the pool's edge and clawing her nails into his arms from climaxing. Her head pressing against his shoulder. Virel drawing harder on the nap of her neck.

Virel felt her vagina vigorously sucking on his cock harder. Gripping tighter on her hips with both hands. Thrusting faster into her sheathe "LIORA MY SMARA!"

gasping as his semen plunged deep into Liora once again. Over filling her womb and leaving him heaving from pure ecstasy. His pelvis came to a slow dance as he towers over her. "Are you okay?" Virel says in a worried tone. "Yes my dear I just need a breather." Virel holds her in his arms as a protective shield.

After finishing drying off with towels and dressing for the rest of the day. Liora knelt beside Virel tending to his mostly healed gash on his arm. "My love, where did you get this?" As she tore a strip from her long white sleeve wrapping it carefully then pressed a soft kiss to the wound.

Virel watched her with a full heart. "I got it while we were fighting the Gashadokuro from earlier."

"You know I was always scared to have sex because my mother always said it would hurt the first time. But oddly enough it wasn't with you."

"In most books here, describe rare women who don't feel pain during their first time. Maybe that's how it is with you but just in case, I'll be more gentle on you for a while."

Virel says in a gentle tone.

A genuine smile spreads across Liora's face.

Virel couldn't help but think to himself: *Choosing her was not wrong. But what does it all mean for the Archive?*

He stood as his face turned serious, now gazing at the wall behind the pool.

There it was.

The newly formed glyph.

Etched in glowing gold pulsing faintly. Unlike anything they'd seen before.

Liora followed his gaze, eyes narrowing.

"Let me grab my notebook," she said. "If I can trace the shape, maybe I can match it to something in the Archive."

She retrieved her notebook flipping to a fresh page, pencil poised.

The glyph shimmered with three interlocking curves, a central flame, and a spiral that pulsed in time with their breath.

Virel stepped closer.

"It's not just a symbol. It looks like a response."

Liora nodded slowly. Not saying another word as Virel continued.

"Maybe a record of choice of transformation."

She traced the lines carefully, her hand steadying, her racing heart.

"It started during the battle," he said quietly. "When I tried to turn into mist, nothing happened. I thought the Gashadokuro was blocking me… but it wasn't."

He moved a little closer.

"It feels like you're pulling me into a solid body. I know it sounds strange, but it's real. You're grounding me, Liora. And I think I'm becoming… human."

Liora paused, her hand still over the glyph. "What does that mean, Virel?"

"I'm not sure," he said, touching her cheek. "But if becoming flesh is what it takes to stay with you… then I'm willing."

Somewhere deep in the Archive, a door suddenly unlocked with a hissing sound as air finally breathed into the open space from within the wall.

# The First Forgotten Catalog

LIORA TRACED THE final curve of the glyph and the door from the chamber seemed to open with a soft groan. Not mechanical but organic like the Archive itself was exhaling. Inside the air was still. Sacred.

Virel stepped in first, his eyes scanning the shelves. The catalogs were unlike anything he'd seen before bound in materials that shimmered between leather and light. Etched with runes that pulsed faintly as he helped Liora into the room while holding her hand.

Walking further in he reached for one.

It didn't resist.

The cover was marked with another symbol he didn't recognize: three intersecting circles, a flame at the center, and a spiral trailing outward. He opened it.

The room responded.

Light flared. The glyphs on the walls pulsed. All of a sudden.

A memory.

Projected in the air before them like mist woven into a story.

A being stood in a chamber much like this one tall, luminous, flickering between forms. They spoke to a mortal woman, her hand resting on their chest.

"I choose you," the being said.

"Even if it unravels me."

The woman wept. Not from fear but from knowing.

The being fractured. The spell cracked and they became something new. The mist like proicere vanish from their sights.

Looking at the final entry in the catalog it was blank.

No ending. No record.

Just a single line etched in gold:

"To choose love is to rewrite the Archive."

Virel stared at the page breath shallowly.

"I don't remember this," he said.

"But I think… I wasn't meant to."

Liora touched the edge of the catalog with her fingers trembling.

"Then maybe this isn't just your story."

"Maybe it's ours."

There was a second catalog that was heavier than the first. Bound in dark leather etched with fractured glyphs. It pulsed faintly with a reddish hue like a warning.

Virel opened it slowly.

Inside there was a record of a being who had tried to choose humanity. The entries were fragmented and erratic. The transformation had begun but something had gone wrong.

The being had loved. Had felt. Had wanted.

But their partner had not trusted them. Had feared the change. Had pulled away.

The final entry was a blank page and scorched at the edges.

Liora's breath caught. Hand over her mouth.

"They didn't make it. Did they?"

Virel nodded his voice low.

"The bond fractured and so did the spell."

They stared at the page in silence, the weight of it settling between them.

Then another glyph shimmered on the back cover. Faint. Dormant.

Until Liora reached out and touched it.

Nothing happened.

Virel placed his hand beside hers. "Best if we leave it alone for…" before he could finish his sentence.

The glyph flared to life.

Purple light surged around them and the wall behind the catalog shelf shifted. A hidden door revealed itself etched with the same symbol that had just awakened.

Three interlocking: circles. A flame. A spiral.

Above it, a single word pulsed in ancient script:

"Trust."

# Entering the Chamber

THEY STEPPED INSIDE together.

The chamber was round, quiet and pulsing with soft purple light. No scrolls. No relics. Just a single pedestal in the center and a mirrored wall that reflected not their bodies but their bond.

Virel saw himself holding Liora's hand. Liora saw herself leaning into him, eyes closed, heart open.

The pedestal held a single object: a crystal orb, swirling with mist and memory.

A voice not spoken but felt echoed through the room:

"Only those who trust may rewrite the Archive."

Virel looked at Liora.

"Do you trust me?"

She nodded as her eyes steady on him.

"With everything."

They reached for the orb together.

And the Archive held its breath.

A blinding blue light surged from the Orb as Virel and Liora touched it together. Then silence.

Virel blinked. Beneath his boots the ground shimmered like glass. Cool and impossibly smooth. He stood on a floating platform suspended in a void of soft azure mist. Below twisting walls of stone and crystal formed a vast maze. Its paths shift subtly like breathing architecture.

"Liora?" he called out, his voice echoing through the chamber.

Down below Liora spun in place, eyes wide, her braid catching the unknown direction of light. She looked up startled and spotted him.

"Virel? How did you get up there?!"

"I woke up here," he replied, scanning the horizon. "Are you alright?!"

"I think so. Just... confused."

A sharp tick... tick... tick... rang out, rhythmic and mechanical. Reverberating through the maze. Virel flinched as it wasn't just below. He could hear it too.

His eyes narrowed. "This must be the Trial of Trust!"

Liora's brow furrowed. "What do we do?!"

Virel stepped to the edge of the glass peering down. He could see that the maze's entrance behind her was sealed shut. No way back. Only forward.

"I think I'm meant to guide you!," he said slowly. "I'll watch over you! Help you through!"

Liora smirked, rolling her shoulders back. "Easy enough. I trust you!"

The ticking continued in a soft whisper.

Virel's voice cut through the echo: "Liora, you're doing great! Just keep moving! I'm watching you, smara!"

She nodded, breath ragged, feet pounding the stone. The maze twisted around her, the walls rising and falling like breath. At that moment a sudden:

CRACK.

The floor behind her split open with a thunderous groan. Liora spun around, eyes wide.

The ticking grew louder, faster. Like a heartbeat on the edge of panic.

From the pitch black chasm, a massive horned figure rose. Its body is carved from shadow and muscle. Eyes glowing like embers.

"Ah! ¡Dios mío!" she screamed! Stumbling backward and moving her hands in a crossing motion.

The Minotaur roared. A sound so deep it vibrated the maze walls and sent tremors through Virel's glass stage above. Dust rained down. The ticking echoed louder. Now tinged with urgency.

"LIORA, RUN!" Virel shouted as he scanned the maze. "I see a path go to the next right, then sharp left!"

She bolted, the Minotaur crashing after her. It's hooves shattering stone, horns scraping walls.

Virel's eyes darted. There he saw it. A narrow corridor veering right and ending in a pit lined with jagged obsidian spikes. The path was barely visible from Liora's angle.

"Liora!" he called. "There's a trap ahead. Take the next left, then right. Make it look like you're cornered."

"WHAT?! ARE YOU CRAZY!!" she gasped, dodging a swipe from the Minotaur's claw.

"TRUST ME! There's a pit. If you time it right and make it look like you're trapped. It'll charge you. You could try to jump right in between its legs"

She hesitated, then whined a bit before nodding at Virel instructions. "OKAY. Okay. Let's do this."

She sprinted down the detour. The Minotaur thundering behind her. The ticking was deafening now. The echoing is like a countdown. Virel clenched his fists as he watched her every turn.

Legs pumping with adrenaline and trying not to skid on the oddly new marble white flooring. Hoping to reach the pit with each turn as the high walls are all made with obsidian glass. Hearing the Minotaur crushing hooves as they rock the solid floor with each step. Making bursts of speed difficult to keep out of reach. The first left nearly missed the large fist break through part of the obsidian wall. Shards exploded across the area, cutting flesh from both Liora and the Minotaur. Luckily though her cuts were small and superficial, compared to the massive amount of damage to the Minotaur hand.

Making a reminder to herself the next route is a right turn at the end of this hallway, bolting to a running sprint to her next location. The Minotaur slows ever so slightly thanks to his dripping blood, sinew dangling from its fist and broken obsidian under its hooves. Creating a weird deformed slip and slide, the monster's heavy breath blasted behind her back. Making it feel like it was a lot closer than it was, smacking lightly against the wall and Liora reached the edge of the pit. Skids to a stop and turned. Her face is full of defiant breaths as they heave from her lungs.

The Minotaur reached the beginning of the hall. Starting right at her with a roared at the challenge and charged forward.

"Now!" Virel shouted.

Instead of jumping between the beast's legs. Liora saw it left a big gap on its right side. So she leapt sideways. Rolling against the wall as the beast barreled forward too fast to stop.

With a final roar. It plunged into the pit impaled on the obsidian spikes below.

Silence.

Then the ticking slowed… softened… and faded.

Virel exhaled. "You did it!"

Liora looked up, as she was still sitting on the floor with eyes wide. Heart pounding and she raised up her thumb in a sign of agreement. For a while she kept wheezing for air but once she got her bearings, she was able to breathe better. They were able to continue their quest to reach the end of this maze.

Liora notices 2 small shadows made from glob forms of human bodies with complete inky solid color. Coming from the small shadows of the maze. They stand around 2' feet tall with black eyes and white lining their edges. Giving them a lifeless look. Their tiny screeches tear through the air. With no weapons beside her. The only way out is past them.

Virel spoke with his infinite knowledge, "Move to make a hard right and continue down without stopping. Whatever you do! DON'T LOOK BACK! They're slow but can paralyzed you with a single swipe!"

"You don't have to tell me twice!" Liora sprinting away from the pit making a hard right and down the hall. The screeches far away but all still so resonating in her bones. An obsidian wall made a movement upward right behind her so quickly that it nudged her forward. This essentially separates her from the shadow monsters. Hopefully her luck has changed.

The maze became awfully quiet.

No more shifting walls. No more ticking. Just the soft hum of stillness like the breath of the world holding steady.

Liora stepped forward, guided by Virel's voice from above. Each turn had been a test, each shadow a threat but now at the heart of the labyrinth, she saw it.

The orb.

It hovered slightly above another pedestal of obsidian glass glowing with the same radiant blue light that had engulfed them before. Familiar. Powerful. Waiting.

She looked up.

Virel finally at the end of the stage stood above hands pressed to the transparent wall, eyes locked on hers.

"Do I take it?! What if I don't see you again!?," she said softly.

"That won't happen! I trust you!," Virel replied. "Go ahead! Take it!"

Liora reached out fingers trembling slightly and grasped the orb.

In an instant the maze dissolved.

She blinked and found herself standing face to face with Virel. He is casting over her as his hand is still on the glass stage wall. It was like he never moved. The glass faded with them no longer separated by glass or distance. The orb pulsed gently in her right hand casting soft blue light across their faces.

They looked at each other for a moment and embraced.

A long, quiet hug. The kind that says we made it. The kind that binds souls.

As Virel's hand slid onto her left breast then gave her a gentle kiss. One that felt grounding and real. Then moving his hands from her breast to her back and down to her ass.

"We now know you prefer both boob and ass. Over hugs." As Liora giggled to herself between their kisses.

Virel gave her a firm squeeze to both of her ass cheeks. With a mischievous grin and Virel hearing Liora moaning into his mouth. Made him crazy with lust. Having their tongues intertwin like a dance. Liora pushed her hips into Virel letting him know how she wanted his touch more. Stopping only to gasp for air. He gives her one more gentle kiss.

Still holding the orb Liora looked up at him, her forehead resting against his. Biting her lower lip she places the orb between their chest.

Her hands already on the orb Virel placed his big hand over hers while touching the orb.

It flared.

Light surged around them once more. Lifting their feet from the ground and dissolving the space between trials.

# Truth or Liar?

TOGETHER THEY VANISHED and the blue light from the orb faded. Virel and Liora find themselves in a vast chamber of still water. The surface is so perfectly smooth it reflects the stars above as though there is no sky. Just silence. Just them.

They step forward holding hands, as the water ripples from underway.

From the ripples two figures arise. Identical in form but not in presence. Virel sees himself but is colder. Sharper. Detached. A version of him that never chose compassion. Liora sees herself but burdened with eyes heavy with doubtful hands stained with blood of regret she never had before.

The ticking returned soft at first then louder. Not from the water but from within them.

Virel's reflection started to make its way forward. Its voice was as harsh and cold as the wind.

"You could've led alone. You didn't need her. You were meant to be more than a guide you were meant to rule."

Virel kept his eyes on his water reflection version. His jaw clenched, eyes remained steady:

"I was meant to remember. To protect. Not to rule over knowledge."

"Then why do you fear being forgotten? Why do you cling to her like she's your anchor?"

Virel quietly saying:

"Because she reminds me I'm more than a memory. She sees me and not just the stories or information I carry."

On the right of Virel, Liora had to deal with her own self. It was circling her to get her to move away from Virel. Her voice sounded like water dripping on stone. So quiet but had a lasting sound to it.

"You're not strong enough. You always need someone to tell you where to go. You're just a follower."

Liora had her fists clenched and then she released them slowly.

"You're right. I am a follower. Just because I follow doesn't make me weak. It means I trust those who are close to me."

"Oh, really? Then why do you doubt yourself every time you're alone? Why do you freeze when no one's watching?"

Liora's voice begins to rise:

"It's because I am afraid of failing. I have no one to turn to. It's just me in this big vast world of darkness."

The ticking slowed.

The reflections flickered, their edges blurring.

Virel walked toward Liora and reached for her hand.

"You're never alone my dear. You have me and we will face everything together."

Their reflections say in unison:

"You can't help each other here. Only truth can pass."

Liora squeezes Virel's hand and in doing so. Virel began to speak to the reflections.

"I fear being forgotten but as time goes on all I've ever done will fade away one day. I'd rather be remembered for love than for power or knowledge."

He says with a soft smile as he looks into Liora's eyes.

Liora nervously says with a small sigh.

"Fine. Fine! I fear I'm not enough. Without someone to guide me, I'd be lost. I know I need to do things myself. It's just taking me a while to trust myself and my ability to persevere."

Virel's reflections smiled softly then dissolved into light. Liora and Virel still see Liora's reflection standing there.

"You are not being truthful." A hissing sound comes from the reflective water form.

Thinking to herself: *I don't understand. I* ***was*** *being truthful and yet she calls me a liar. Maybe one of us has to say our truth and the other lies. I don't understand, the word "trust" was on the door before entering. There is so much that could be implemented. Oh, I hope I am not totally wrong by doing this. Please forgive me my love if I'm wrong.*

Giving Virel a small pleading look before she shouted at her own reflection.

"No shit I wasn't. This isn't my therapy session!"

"Liora? What are you doing?" Virel looks at Liora nervously.

"I'm about to beat my own ass! This is what's about to happen." She says as she gives a quick look at Virel full of frustration.

Its lingered eyes, dark and wild. Its lips curled into a sinister smile.

"You're a liar," it shrilled. "You don't trust yourself. You never did."

Before either of them could react the reflection lunged its cold slick hands. Wrapping around Liora's neck then dragging her beneath the water's surface.

Virel shouted, "Liora!"

He dove toward her but the water resisted him. His fists struck the surface but it rippled like the glass from before, like it was unbreakable. He could see her struggling below bubbles rising, her eyes closed and her panic in her movements.

"Let her go!" he roared, punching again and again.

The ticking returned louder now echoing like a countdown to loss.

At that moment he saw it.

The orb.

Floating just behind him a pulsing light resting on the water's surface like a beacon.

Virel turned, grabbed it and without hesitation. Sprinting back to the reflection. As it cackles at Liora drowning below them.

"You want the truth?" he growled. "Here's mine!"

The reflection looked in his direction for a moment before he smashed the orb into the reflection's face.

The water exploded as soon as the orb touched it.

Liora burst through the surface, gasping for air, coughing, eyes wild and wet.

Virel was already there with his arms outstretched. He caught her lifting her into his arms. Bridal carrying her and holding her close to his chest.

"Don't worry, love," he whispered in a steady voice. "I got you."

She clung to him breathing harshly but coming to a slow pace with him, as their heartbeat synced with each other.

The chamber was still.

Virel carried Liora across the water-like floor, her body trembling soaked and breathless. The orb pulsed faintly in his hand, its light dimmed but steady. They reached the far edge of the chamber where the water no longer touched the ground.

He knelt down cradling her in his arms. Letting her catch her breath.

Liora's voice was barely dribbling. "She said I was a liar."

Virel brushed a strand of wet hair from her face. "She was fear and what she said was not the truth."

"But I do doubt myself," she says while looking into his eyes. "I say I'm strong but sometimes I don't believe it. I feel like I'm pretending."

Virel leaned his forehead against hers. "There is a reason why people say fake it until you make it, baby. It's survival. You kept moving. That's strength."

She closed her eyes, tears mixing with the water on her cheeks. "She knew exactly where to strike and it cut me real deep. Also, did you just make a pun?"

"I guess I did.," he said softly with a warm smile.

Liora opened her eyes again and giggled ever so lightly. "Wait, Why didn't your reflection stay?"

Virel looked down at the orb. "Maybe because I've already drowned in my doubts for so long that this time I believed you more than I feared myself."

She smiled faintly then reached up and touched his cheek. "You saved me."

"Always," in a gruff voice.

They sat there for a moment longer wrapped in silence with the orb glowing between them.

Then the chamber shifted once again as a soft wind passed, a ripple in the water starts to evaporate, a whisper of the next trial calling.

Virel was still holding her in his arms and she didn't protest.

"Ready?" he asked.

Liora nodded. "With you always."

# To New Beginnings

Touching the new orb they are sent to a twilight realm split by a river of memory. Virel and Liora are cast into opposite banks. Unable to see or reach each other due to the distance. The invisible walls themselves breathed with a light turquoise color. Each inscription is carved deep into the walls. Each line shimmered with the same command: Sacrifice what you hold most dear. Speak the vow. Survive the collapse. If both choose self preservation the river floods and they are cast adrift. If one sacrifices and the other does not. The bond frays but survives. If both sacrifice the river parts and the pair reunites.

Virel pressed his palm against the wall. In his other hand holds the orb pulsed faintly as though he knew what was coming. His jaw tightened.

"I give up my bond to the Temple of Knowledge," he whispered with conviction. "I give up my immortality."

With a sharp motion he smashed the orb into the wall that's separating him from the river. It shattered like crystal, turquoise veins racing outward from the impact. His right arm starts to get turquoise like veins, just like the wall.

On the opposite side Liora felt this strange pull. She placed her trembling hand against the wall as she whispered:

"I give up time. I give up my past, not just my present, all of it. For the man I love."

The wall drank her words. The river between them split open parting like a wound in the earth.

They ran to each other, arms outstretched, colliding in an embrace. Only for the floor to give way beneath them.

CRACK

They hear the walls crackling before they could react. They fell as the Darkness swallowed everything.

When their eyes opened again. They stood in the main chamber. The temple groaned like a dying beast. The splitting of the walls' turquoise veins glowing brighter and brighter until they looked ready to burst. Even Virel's right arm starts to glow.

Virel staggered clutching his chest. "I feel it… I'm being freed."

But the freedom came with a weight.

Not pain, just one of recognition.

A memory, ancient and buried, surged through him like the full concentration of the Sun. Not his memory.

The man.

The conduit.

Memories rushing too fast for him to grasp like a tsunami. Glimpses appear to be clearer. The one who had stood behind the silver eyed woman. Silent, steady and offering his soul to the spell as a kick start, that would forge Virel's body. His death in the fire had not been the end. But a merging of his soul. That had not fully passed on. It laid dormant curled like a seed in Virel's soul core. The silver eye woman offers a red substance along each of the glyphs. Before he could see more. A large quaking motion disruptes his vision.

Now with the temple breaking. The old bindings unraveling that soul stirred.

Virel grabs hold of what little vision flickering in his mind. He saw the woman. Not as a spirit but now as Liora. Her voice. Her eyes. The way she stood when she was angry. The way she reached for him when she thought he wasn't looking.

*Could it be?*

*Could she be the same soul, just reborn?*

The thought struck him like a bell. Not with fear but with hope. A thread pulled taut across lifetimes drawing them together again.

He looked at her, really took in her face and for a moment in time, felt like it had stopped.

Maybe they were always meant to find each other.

Maybe this was the shape love took when it refused to die.

Liora shook her head. "I feel no different at all. Hey what's that on your–"

Stones start to rain down upon them. The turquoise veins shattered like glass releasing a sound like moans from the deep earth. Speaking all across the temple as man made glyphs glow with a bright white light.

"We got to get out of here!" Virel seized her hand, pulling them into a desperate sprint. They slid beneath a falling boulder, ducked across rubble and burst through the collapsing archway just as the temple roared behind them.

Outside they collapsed to their knees. Coughing through dust and smoke. The mountain wind whipped around them carrying the last echoes of the temple's despair from collapse. When the air cleared they turned towards the mountain's edge.

Which stretched vast and empty, neither past nor future Liora could name. "This doesn't seem right. I don't see the road, light poles or aircraft warning lights." Knowing something didn't add up.

They turned back expecting to see ruins, rubble, or some trace of what they had endured.

But there was nothing.

The mountainside was smooth, unbroken stone, as if no temple had ever stood there at all. No turquoise veins, no shattered walls, only silence.

Looking back once more at the horizon.

They stood together on the edge of the mountain, hands still clasped together. Staring into a world that was both ending and beginning

Virel's chest rose and fell with a strange calm. "I am free," with an unwavering voice. Though the weight of centuries had finally been lifted.

Liora's gaze swept the horizon. "And I… am unmoored."

The world before them was wrong. No villages. No tracks. No planes overhead. Her satellite phone glowed with a full battery but not a single signal. The horizon light was descending in a purplish-red color almost as if their day was coming to a close. The trees sway slightly from the warm breeze as their Fuchsia and Amaranth leaves dance in the wind. The River from the distance had a beautiful glow of a clear Cherry blossom pink. It was as if you could see the contrasting colors of the vibrate fish in there.

Whispering almost to herself:

"I didn't give up my memories. I gave up, time."

As she looked into Virel's eyes. Her words hung between them like a curse.

Virel looked at her: "This doesn't look like our world dear but whatever happens I'm with you always."

For a heartbeat the air shimmered. Liora's eyes soften to his words and a gentle smile comes across her face. Virel turquoise veins flickering faintly across his arm. A sound rose from the mountain's depths not quite a groan, not quite a sigh but something older something was watching them.

They stood together bound by vow and sacrifice. Though the temple is gone now. Its shadow lingered waiting, patient, as if their trials was not an ending at all but the first in a game yet to be revealed.

Whatever had changed they would face it side by side. As Virel gives her a soft kiss on her hands.

*The End*

www.ingramcontent.com/pod-product-compliance
Lightning Source LLC
LaVergne TN
LVHW090617110826
845146LV00001B/433

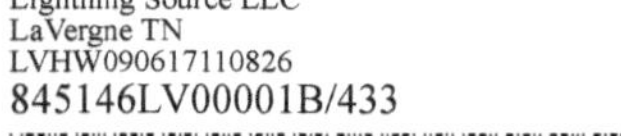

* 9 7 9 8 9 9 5 2 1 7 4 0 4 *